P9-DNL-160

GONE FISHING

a novel in verse

By Tamera Will Wissinger

Illustrated by Matthew Cordell

HOUGHTON MIFFLIN
Houghton Mifflin Harcourt

Houghton Mifflin Books for Children is an imprint of
Houghton Mifflin Harcourt Publishing Company.

www.hmhbooks.com

The text of this book is set in Bodoni, ScalaSans, and Kidprint.
The illustrations are pen and ink with watercolor.

"Night Crawlers" first published in *Wee Ones* magazine, 2007.
(September, 2007, one time electronic rights.)

Library of Congress Cataloging-in-Publication Data
Wissinger, Tamera Will.
Gone fishing : a novel / by Tamera Will Wissinger.
pages cm
Summary: In this novel told through poems, nine-year-old Sam loves fishing with his dad, so when his pesky little sister horns in on their fishing trip, he is none too pleased. Inludes primer on rhyme, poetry techniques, rhythm, stanzas, and poetic forms.
ISBN 978-0-547-82011-8
[1. Novels in verse. 2. Fishing–Fiction. 3. Brothers and sisters–Fiction.] I. Title.
PZ7.5.W57Go 2013
[Fic]–dc23
2012032796

Manufactured in the United States of America
DOC 10 9 8 7 6 5 4 3 2 1
4500398553

To my parents, Joanne and Clayton Will,
who took their family fishing, and still do.
They inspired this story.

With love,
T.W.W.

CONTENTS

Sam

NIGHT CRAWLERS

Tercet Variation

Dark night.
Flashlight.
Dad and I hunt worms tonight.

Grass slick.
Worms thick.
Tiptoe near and grab them quick.

Hold firm.
They squirm.
Tug-o-war with earth and worm.

Ninety-four.
Worms galore.
Set our bucket near the door.

Next day.
No delay.
Look out, fish — we're on our way!

Sam

JUST DAD AND ME

Free Verse Poem

For fishing tomorrow
it's just us two.
Not Mom, not Grandpa,
                                        not Lucy.
It'll be like playing catch or
painting the garage.
Just Dad and me.
Fishing.

SAM

Sam

MY TACKLE BOX

Switcheroo Poem

I love my fishing tackle box — it's green and blue and gold.
My grandpa gave it to me when I wasn't very old.

I need to get it ready for tomorrow at the lake.
We're leaving in the morning just as soon as we're awake.

One tiny *click* and now my treasure chest is open wide.
A shelf with lots of little spaces holds my gear inside.

My silver sinkers, wiggle worms, my floating frogs, my line.
My shiny spinner lures, my bobbers, hooks — there're twenty-nine.

The shelf is on a hinge — it hides my secret space below.
It's where I keep my special treasures out of sight —

OH NO! . . .

Where's my compass?
Where's my map?
Where's my lucky fishing cap?

Where's my stringer?
Something's wrong!

This *princess doll* does not belong!

POW

What is this?

A throne?
A crown?
A polka-dotted circus clown?
A tiny bottle of *perfume*?

I smell *Lucy* in my room!

Lucy

FISHING FOR PRETEND

Dramatic Poem for One, Quatrains

Oh, Sam — you're here. Come on, let's play!
I'm fishing for pretend tonight.
It's fun to use your gear this way.
Hold on, I think I have a bite.

Your map's a paper fishing boat.
Your compass is the steering wheel.
I think our boat could really float.
It would be fun to fish for real.

Your stringer makes a tiny lake.
I didn't crumple up your map.
Your compass works — it didn't break.
I sure do like your fishing cap.

I didn't snoop — I made a trade.
Stay here, sit down, don't go away.
Don't you like the boat I made?
Your fishing stuff is fun — come play!

Sam

A FISHY SPELL

Curse Poem, Poem of Address

May a worm crawl up your nose,
    Leeches creep between your toes.

May your nails be caked with dirt.
    May a bug fly up your skirt.

May your birthday gifts be coal.
    May you smell like a dirty troll.

May you step in gooey muck
    And for days be frozen stuck.

May a seagull dive and swoop
    And drop a bombshell in your soup.

May you grow a knee-length beard
    So your friends all think you're weird.

If you ever take my gear
    May your bones quake, *SAM IS NEAR.*

Sam

a

w

a

k

e.

THE NIGHT BEFORE FISHING

Concrete Poem, Parody Poem

wide

'Tis I'm

the and

night fishing

before

day

of best

fishing let my

arrive. oh please

p

l

e

a

s

e

Wonder
how
many
fish
I will
catch
at the
lake.
Could
be
nine.
Maybe
twelve?
Seventeen?
Twenty-five?

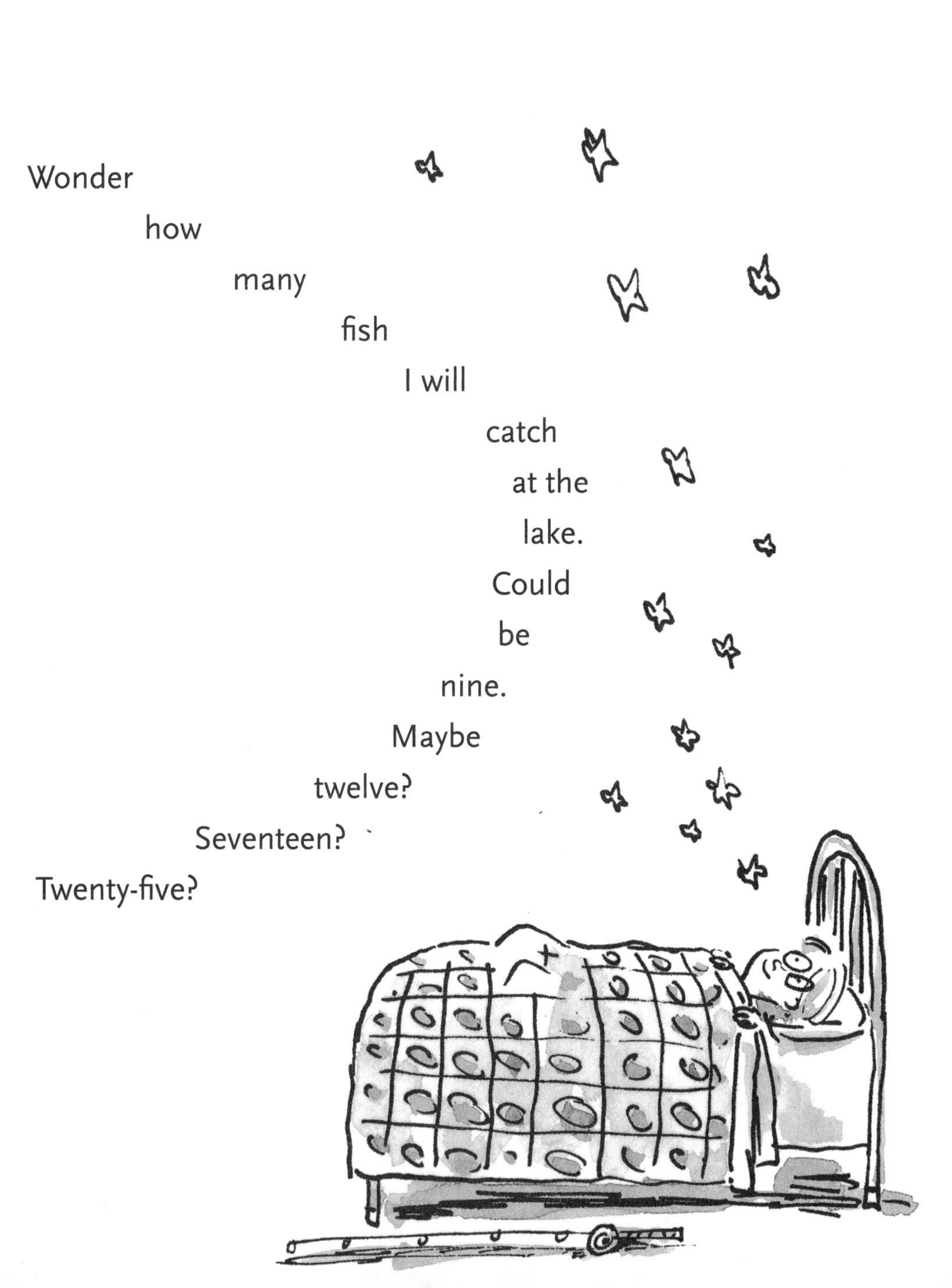

GONE
FISHING

Sam

GONE FISHING

Couplets

Hip-hip, hooray!
It's fishing day.

Yo-ho, yippee!
Just Dad and me.

My fishing gear
Is all right here.

Hello there, moon.
I'm fishing soon.

Can hardly wait
To throw my bait.

I think for fun
I'll catch a ton.

It's fishing day.
I'm on my way.

My door sign's swishing:

I've GONE FISHING.

Sam, Dad, and Lucy

UP AND AT 'EM

Dramatic Poem for Three

Sam	*Dad*
Dad, wake up! It's six-o-eight.	
	It's dark outside; the fish will wait.
I'll make toast, I'll pack the truck,	
Load our worms—they'll bring us luck.	
	Okay, I'm up. I'll help you load
	So we can get out on the road.
	I guess.
	There's room for both of you.
But Lucy took my fishing gear.	
Maybe she should stay right here.	
Plus she likes to twirl and play.	
She'll scare all the fish away!	
	Sam's right, we can't play games or jump . . .

Lucy

A fishing trip?

Can I go too?

Sam *Dad*

The boat's no place to stomp
or thump.

Okay, then, now it's just us three.

But, Dad, it was just you and me.

I'm sorry, Sam, us three today.
Let's load and we'll be on our way.

Lucy

I won't dance, I won't squirm.
I'll be as quiet as a worm.

Yippee! Hold on. I'll be right back.
I have some fishing stuff to pack.

Sam

CAN'T GO FISHING YET BLUES

Blues Poem

Can't go fishing yet –
    till Lucy packs her stuff.

Doubt she's bringing any
    handy fishing stuff.

I've been waiting fifteen minutes — long enough!

The truck is loaded.
    Why am I still here?

The boat is hitched,
    so why am I still here?

'Cause Lucy is
        the
            Slowpoke
                of
                    the
                        Year . . .

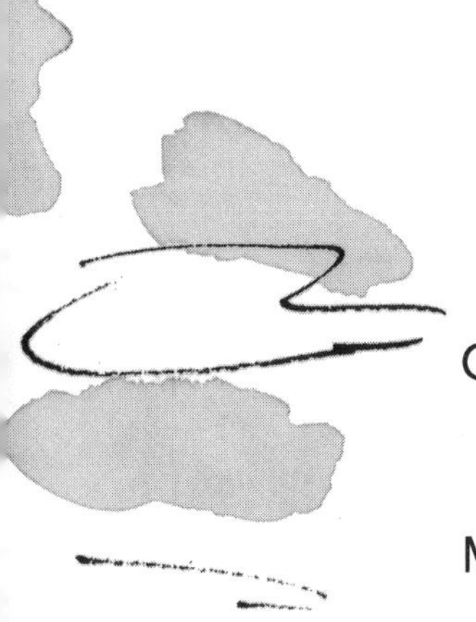

Our boat's not wet and I'm not fishing:
GRRRR.

My line's not wet and I'm not fishing:
GRRRRR.

If I'm skunked today
I'll put the blame on *HER.*

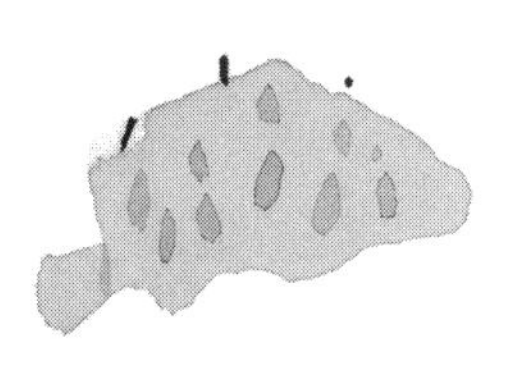

ROCKS

Lucy

WHAT TO PACK?

List Poem

What to pack?
I'll need a snack:
Apple juice, granola bar.

Puzzles, games,
my teddy, James,
My nature books, my toy guitar,

My wooden box
of pretty rocks,
My art supplies—that's *all* I'll take.

I can't forget
my Play-Doh set.
Sam! Aren't you ready for the lake?

Sam

ON THE ROAD

Double Dactyl

Finally, Lucy completed her
Packing — at
Last we are all on the
Road to the lake.

Now if the fish will bite
Overabundantly,
Bringing her won't have been
One big mistake.

GO FISH

Sam and Lucy

I SEE SOMETHING

Dramatic Poem for Two

Sam	*Lucy*
Row	
after row	
of corn, corn, corn,	
CORN!	
	Beans, beans, beans,
	BEANS!
I see something . . .	
	Something green?
I see corn.	
	I see beans.
Corn, corn.	
	Beans, beans.
Look — a farm with sheep!	
	And cows!
A spotted pony by the barn —	
	A teeny-tiny jumping pony.
I'm going to catch a jumping fish . . .	

Sam	*Lucy*
A fighting fish — exciting fish.	
I see something big and blue!	I see something big and blue!
Watch out, fish!	
We're coming through!	We're coming through!

GO FISH

SNACK

Sam

BOAT LAUNCH

Narrative Poem Variation

We made it to the lake — hurray!
Let's launch the boat.

We stand beside the snack bar.
Soon our boat will float.

Dad eases down the launch ramp
when the way is clear.

The trailer tires splash the lake.
and disappear.

A seagull swoops, cries out,
then settles on a rock.

Our boat is launched. Dad ties it
tightly to the dock.

He parks the truck and trailer,
whistles out a tune.

It's time to load the boat —
we'll all be fishing soon!

Sam

ALL ABOARD!

List Poem

Fishing poles,
My tackle box,
Extra pairs of shoes and socks,
Our sweatshirts and
The camera bag,
The fishing net,
The boating flag,
Suntan lotion,
Baseball caps,
Lucy's backpack,
Boating maps,
The worms we found outside last night,
Our safety vests, fastened tight,
Lunch and
Drinking water, too.
Next it's time to load the crew.
Lucy's first.
I'm last onboard.
All our gear is neatly stored.

We take our seats.
Dad turns the key.
The motor growls.
The ropes are free.
My compass helps us navigate.
Dad is captain.
I'm first mate.
We push off slowly,
Leave no wake.
Here we go —
Across the lake!

Sam

CROSSING THE LAKE

Free Verse Poem

Wave
Over wave
Over wave,
We sway at the bow
As Dad steers the boat
Across the lake.
Mist sprinkles our arms in
Dewy
Drops
That glisten in the sun.
Rainbows
Flicker and fade,
Flicker
And
Fade
With each spray.
Wind blows aboard,
Whisks our hair,

Then glides away

As Dad slows the boat

And steers toward

Our

Lucky

Fishing

Spot.

Sam

FISHERMAN'S PRAYER

Prayer Poem

Send me a fish that is lively and long.
One that is sturdy, stupendous, and strong.

Maybe a walleye, a catfish or two —
Even a perch or a bluegill will do.

Now is the moment. I'm up to the task.
Any fish, many fish, that's all I ask.

Sam

RECIPE FOR FISHING

How-To Poem

Ingredients:

1 anchor, dropped and tied

3 fishing poles with reels and line

3 worms

3 hooks

3 bobbers

3 sinkers

1 cookie each

Directions:

Pluck worm from pail.

Jiggle in front of sister's nose.

Tell her "Shhh!" if she squeals.

Fasten worm to hook.

Be careful not to poke fingers.

Clip favorite bobber to line.

Add silver sinker to keep worm from floating up.

Look around to make sure way is clear.

Click reel, swing pole back,

Then forward, lift thumb.

Wait for fish to bite.

Sam

WHEN WE'RE FISHING

Quatrain

When we're fishing, we talk softly so we don't scare fish away.

When we're fishing, we move gently so the boat won't tip or sway.

When we're fishing, we watch closely that we haven't lost our bait.

But mostly, when we're fishing we must

wait

and wait

and wait.

Sam

FIRST CATCH

Lyric Poem

I wish a fish
        I wish a fish
                I wish a fish would bite.

I hope I catch
        I hope I catch
                A fish before tonight.

I think I feel
        I think I feel
                I think I feel a tap.

I reel it in,
        I see a fin,
                And then I catch

                        A cap.

CRINKLE-CRUNCH!
ZIP!
SLAM!
SNACK!

Sam

LUCY'S QUIET TIME

Complaint Poem

She rattles her backpack and
takes out a snack.
She crinkles the wrapping and
crumples the sack.

She crunches and munches and
dribbles her crumbs.
She slurps from her juice box;
she whistles and hums.

She opens her books and
she reads to us all.
She waves to the birds and
she squawks out a call.

She reels and then squeals when
she tangles her line.
She plops out her bobber —
it bobbles with mine.

She cannot be quiet.
It's worse than I feared.
This day would be perfect if . . .

. . . she disappeared.

Sam

LUCY'S SONG

Poem of Address Variation

"Heeere, fishy, fishy, fishy.
Tasty worms for lunch today.
Heeere, fishy, fishy, fish."
While Lucy sings we fish the bay.

I whisper, "Please be quiet.
If we're noisy, fish won't bite."
Then her bobber ducks and jiggles.
Lucy stands and holds on tight.

"It's a nice one, Lucy, sweetheart.
Keep your tip up, set your hook."
Dad jumps up and grabs the net.
I keep fishing. I don't look.

"This one liked my fishy singing."
Lucy reels her first fish in.
Dad says, "Quick, let's get a picture."
Lucy gives a silly grin.

Dad says, "Put it in the lake.
Set it free, and make a wish."
Lucy lets her first fish go.
I wish *I* had caught that fish.

Heeere, fishy, fishy, fishy.
I repeat it quietly.
Heeere, fishy, fishy, fish.
It worked for Lucy — why not me?

Lucy

CATCHING FISH IS SUCH A BLAST!

Triolet

Catching fish is such a blast!
It's easy and I'm really good.
Hooked one on my second cast.
Catching fish is such a blast!
Maybe I'll beat Sam — at last.
I wonder if he thinks I could.
Catching fish is such a blast!
It's easy and I'm really good.

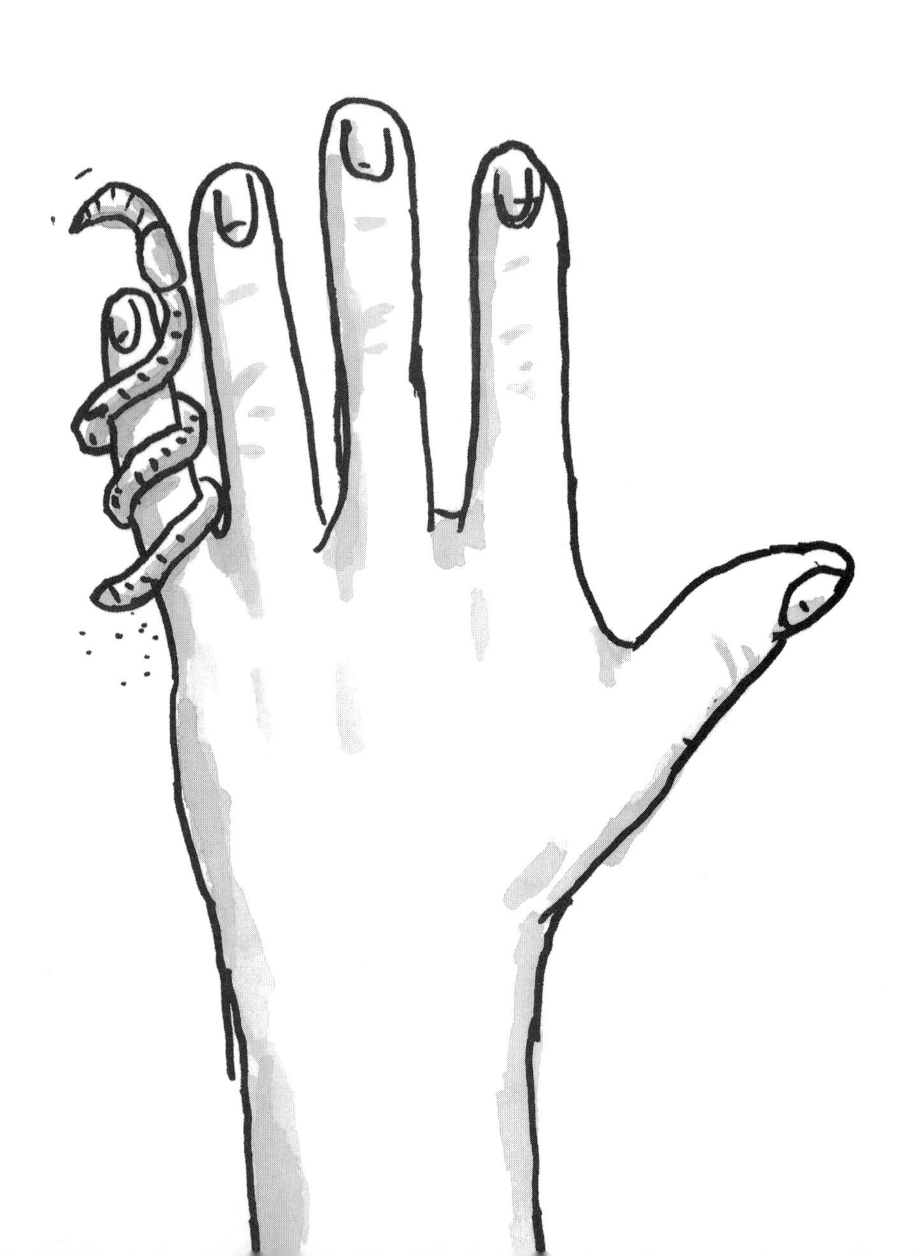

Lucy

FOR THE LOVE OF HAROLD, BEST OF THE WORMS

Ode

First from the bucket of plump worms —

I'll call you Harold.

Chubby, wiggly Harold,

I can't fish

with you!

I pick another and another to catch my bluegills.

And I do, I do!

Lucky Harold!

You curl to sleep

Around my pinky —

Ahh, look at my gorgeous ring!

You want to creep.

up my hand,

up,

Up,

Across my wrist

Until . . .

The worm pail gets low.

Oh, what to do?

Harold.

Sleepy, creeping Harold.

You're a fun worm,

But . . .

Time to work.

Be *de*-licious!

Let's catch a fish!

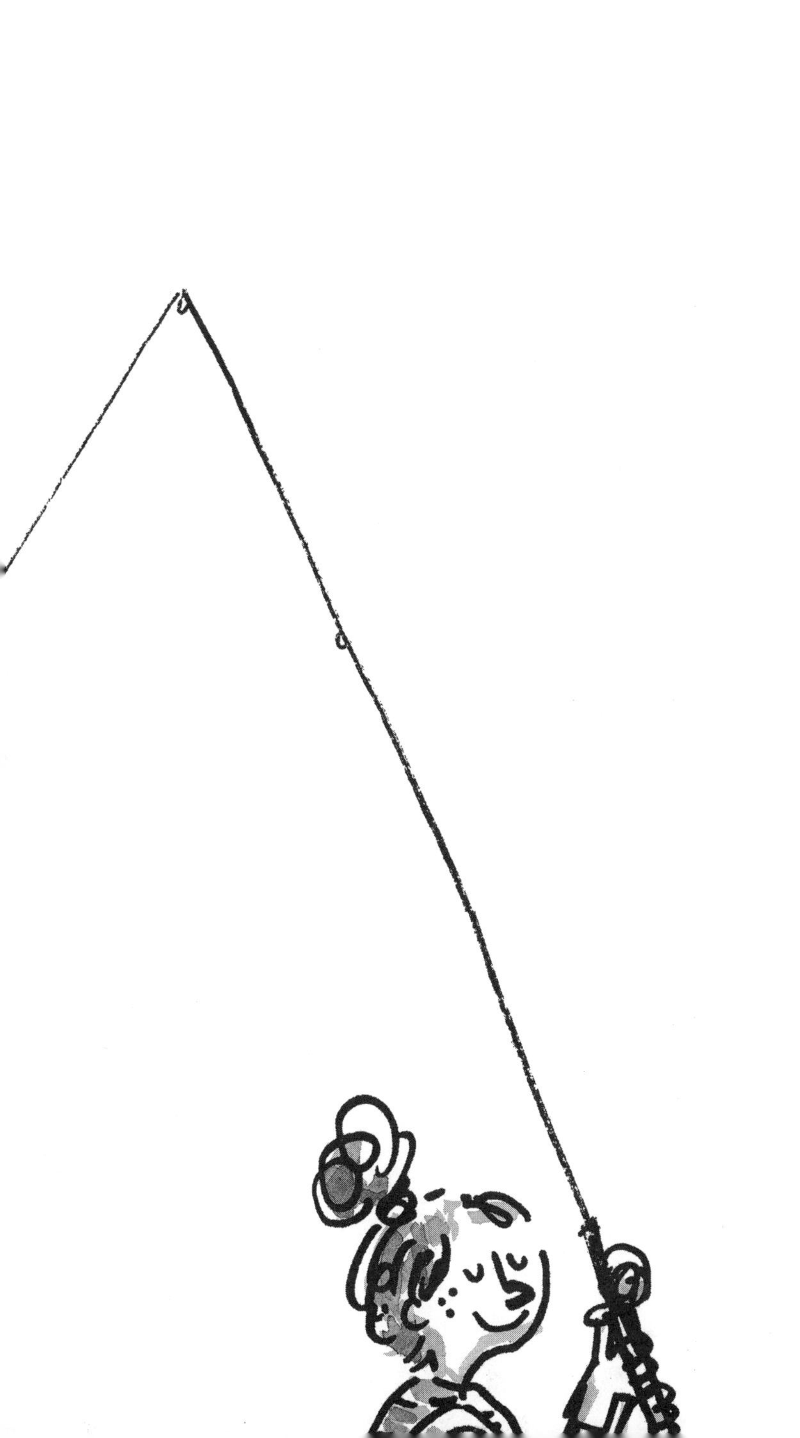

Sam

FISHING SCORE

Counting Poem

One.

Two.

Three.

Four.

Lucy counts her fishing score.

Five.

Six.

Seven.

Eight.

Plus, she's using all the bait.

Eight.

Seven.

Six.

Five.

When will *my* fish arrive?

Four.

Three.

Two.

One.

Lucy's winning eight to . . .

none.

Sam

MY BIG FISH

Quatrains

"Look! My bobber's underwater!
Something's tugging on my line."
"Set your hook and hold your tip up,"
Dad says. "Sam, you're doing fine."
I stand up and tug right back.
Turn the handle of my reel.
Twisting,
lifting,
reeling,
pulling.
Fish is fighting for his meal.
This must be the biggest fish
That anyone has ever caught.
Now my arms are getting tired.
Fish are stronger than I thought.
Water ripples.
It's so close.
I can see its tail
flip
flap.
Dad is ready with the net
One more pull, we'll have it . . .

SNAP!

Bobber flies above my shoulder.
Water makes an arcing spray.
I sure would have liked to see it:

My big fish that got away.

SNAP!

Sam

FISHING FLOP

Ballad

Maybe fishing's not my sport.
        Maybe I don't care.
Maybe I'll try soccer or
        hit golf balls through the air.
Maybe I'll start bowling.
        Maybe I'll shoot hoops.
Maybe I'll run marathons
        or try to skateboard . . . Oops!
Maybe I should watch my pole.
        Maybe that's a bite.
Maybe I should set my hook
        and reel with all my might.
Now my heart is pounding, "Catch it!
        Catch it!" in my chest.
Then I stand and face my fish.
        I need to do my best.
Now we battle like before.
        It zigzags, darts, and weaves.
I fight back — I want to see
        this fish before it leaves . . .

Tug-of-war for minutes, maybe
hours, I don't know.
Long enough to wear us out —
we both seem lazy, slow.
Now my fish makes one last run.
I lift and draw it near.
Dad is ready with the net.
Lucy starts to cheer.
It's a catfish — what a catch!
I smile and pose for Dad.
"It's a keeper, Sam," he says.
A *keeper?* I'm SO GLAD!
Glad I wasn't skunked today.
Glad it picked my bait.
Glad we'll eat it up tonight —
My mouth can hardly wait.
Maybe fishing's kind of fun.
Maybe I'll be back.
Maybe I can catch some more.
Now I have the knack!

Sam

CATFISH SAM

Acrostic Poem

Caught a CATFISH!

Amazing Animal

Torpedo Tough

Fearless Fighter

Intense

Striker

Head Honcho of the Water

Satisfied

Angling

Master

Sam

CATFISH STRONG!

Rondelet

I'm catfish strong!

I caught that lunker. Yee-haw! Wham!

I'm catfish strong!

I could have wrestled all day long.

A catfish wrangler's what *I* am.

That's why they call me Catfish Sam.

I'm catfish strong!

Sam

GULP

Free Verse Poem

"You caught one, Sam!"
Lucy scoots close to me.
"A big one, too!"

I nod, gulp.

I didn't even *look*
when she caught
her first fish.

But she
cheered for me.

Maybe I was wrong
about bringing her along.

Dad

WINNER! WINNER!

Sestet

Winner! Winner! Fish for dinner.

One more cast–it's getting late.

Winner! Winner! Fish for dinner.

Good job, first and second mates.

Winner! Winner! Fish for dinner.

Let's head home to celebrate!

Sam

HOOKED

List Poem

A boat.
A lake.
A fishing team —
My dad, my sister, me.

A launch.
A ride across the lake.
A fishy recipe.

A worm.
A bobber, rod, and reel.
We whispered, waited, looked.

A hope.
A wish.
A fighting fish.
I'm the one who's hooked.

Lucy

A BIG SURPRISE

Couplets

Grandpa! Mom! We have a big surprise!
We've brought a feast — can you believe your eyes?

I caught a lot of bluegills — eight in all.
I let five go 'cause they were pretty small.

But three were keepers — see their gills and tails,
their fanlike fins and tiny, shiny scales?

And Sam caught something too — a great big cat!
I've never seen a kitty look like that.

Show them what you caught — he's giant-size.
Sam and Mr. Whiskers win first prize!

Sam

AMENDS

Cinquain, Forgiveness Poem

Lucy

shows everyone

how I caught my catfish.

My heart hip-hops when she calls me

"hero."

Sam

WHAT CAT IS THAT?

Riddle Poem

What has whiskers, spots, a grin,
Fork tail, no legs, no fur — just skin?

What eats worms and likes to swim,
Is gray, can jump, is long and slim?

What has spiny prickly fins?
Be careful — they can poke like pins.

That is why, unlike a pup,
This cat's not one to cuddle up.

Answer: A catfish!

Dad

NEXT TIME

Limerick

Once a dad took his daughter and son
to catch fish — and they did — what a run!
The daughter caught eight fish.
The son fought two great fish.
So next time, could Dad catch just one?

Dad, Sam, and Lucy

WE LOVE FISHING

Dramatic Poem for Three

Dad

Catfish Sam, hold up your monster fish
and stand by Lucy — wow!

Bluegill Lucy, grab the stringer.
Show your fish off — holy cow!

Those are four amazing fish —
you two look like fishing pros.

Stand up straight, look this way,
and give me your best fishing pose.

When I count three, say, *We love fishing!*
Here we go:

One.

Two.

Three.

Got it! Now just one more shot.
This time it'll be with me.

Grandpa's going to take our picture.
Let me squeeze between you two.

One.

Two.

Three:

Sam	*Dad*	*Lucy*
WE LOVE FISHING!	WE LOVE FISHING!	WE LOVE FISHING!
We're		
	the	
		best
fishing crew!	fishing crew!	fishing crew!

Sam

OUR TAKE

Haiku

Four on a stringer.
Lucy's bluegills, my catfish —
Gold-star fishing day.

Sam

CLEANUP

Reprise Poem, Tercet Variation

Porch light.
Bug bite.
Dad and I clean fish tonight.

Scales slick.
Bluegill thick.
Hold the tail. Be steady, quick.

One more.
Mine makes four.
Wipe the table. Mop the floor.

Full tray.
Fresh fillet.
Grandpa's grill, we're on our way!

Sam

FISH SUPPER

Menu Poem

BEVERAGES

Root Beer or Lemonade (One of each for me.)

APPETIZER

Chips and Salsa (I dumped them in bowls.)

MAIN DISH

Catfish a la Sam (That means I caught it.)

And

Lucy's Juicy Bluegills (Caught by you-know-who.)

SIDES

Corn on the Cob (Grilled by Grandpa.)

And

Potatoes with Onion (Grandpa grilled those, too.)

Watermelon Wedges (Sliced by Dad.)

DESSERT

Angel Food Cake with Strawberry Sauce

(Mom grew the strawberries and baked the cake.)

BEST MEAL *EVER!*

Sam

JUST US THREE

Free Verse Poem, Reprise Poem

For fishing today
it was just us three.
Dad, me,
and Lucy.

I was Dad's right-hand guy.
Lucy was Dad's left-hand gal.
I navigated to our lucky fishing spot,
she sang to the fish.

Dad, Lucy, and me —
just us three.
Fishing.

Sam

FISH TALES

Lyric Poem

I caught a great big fish today and
Lucy caught the most.

Her fish were pretty little,
but I don't want to boast.

My fish was long — from here to there.
It must've weighed a ton.

I tried to catch a lot, but
Lucy beat me eight to one.

I helped when Grandpa grilled our meal.
We ate by lantern light.

The fish was juicy, soft, and warm.
I gobbled every bite.

I hummed while Lucy taught us how
to sing her fishing song.

Next time we're going fishing I hope
she can come along.

THE POET'S TACKLE BOX

Like Sam and his tackle box, poets have a box of tools to help them write poems. Those tools include rhyme, rhythm, poetry techniques, and poetic forms.

In fishing, if one type of bait or approach isn't working, the fisherman or fisherwoman may try something else. This also is true for poets. If you are writing a poem and get stuck, try another form, or try a new topic. (Or take a break. Doing something different for a while may help you get back on track.) Sometimes many poems will appear quickly, as the eight fish do for Lucy. Other times, a poem will appear like Sam's fish—only after you wait and wait. Maybe that poem, like Sam's fish, will be a keeper.

In fishing and in writing, I wish you the best.

—Tamera

RHYME

Rhyme is when syllables, usually at the ends of words, sound exactly the same, such as *night* and *light* or *worm* and *squirm*. Part of the fun and challenge of being a poet is to find rhyming words that work best in a poem, instead of using words that just happen to rhyme. Some poems have very few rhyming words and some poems don't have any.

RHYTHM

Rhythm in poetry is how the words naturally sound when they are read. We emphasize the stress on some syllables and minimize the stress on others. For example, in the words *suppLIES* and *the BOAT,* the emphasis is on the second of the two syllables. In the words *SINGing* and *TRUCK is,* the first syllable of two is stressed. In the words *sevenTEEN* and *twenty-FIVE,* the third syllable of three is emphasized, and the words *NAVigate* and *MANy fish* have a stress on the first syllable of three. Some poems have set rhythm patterns and others don't. Either way, poets notice rhythm and how their words sound with each other.

POETRY 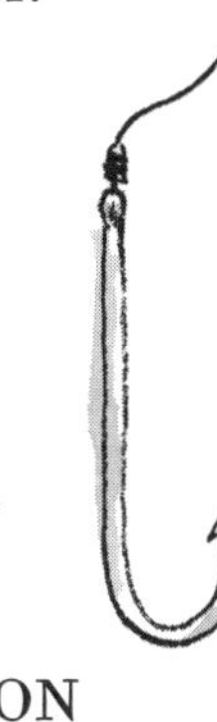 TECHNIQUES

ALLITERATION

Alliteration is the repetition of the same vowel or consonant sound at the beginning of words. The first stanza of "Fisherman's Prayer" has two examples of alliteration: *lively/long* and *sturdy/stupendeous/strong.* "Catfish Sam" also has examples of this technique. Alliteration is a way for the poet to grab the reader's attention.

ANAPHORA

Using a word or a phrase over and over to make a point is anaphora. In "Fishing Flop," the word *maybe* repeats at the beginning of the poem to show Sam's frustration. The word *glad* repeats near the end to show his joy. Anaphora is also used in "First Catch."

APOSTROPHE

Talking directly to a subject that can't respond is apostrophe. In "Gone Fishing," Sam says, "Hello there, moon. I'm fishing soon." Apostrophe is the technique used in poems of address such as "Lucy's Song," and "A Fishy Spell."

ASSONANCE

Assonance is the repetition of a vowel sound within some words in a poem. In "What Cat Is That?," the ĭ sound in all these words creates assonance: *grin/skin/swim/slim/fins/pins.* Sometimes this is called vowel rhyme, and it can be used in words that may or may not rhyme.

HYPERBOLE

Hyperbole is a word or phrase that stretches the truth to make a point. In "Can't Go Fishing Yet Blues," "Lucy is the slowpoke of the year" is hyperbole. It also occurs in "Fish Tales" when Sam says his fish "must've weighed a ton."

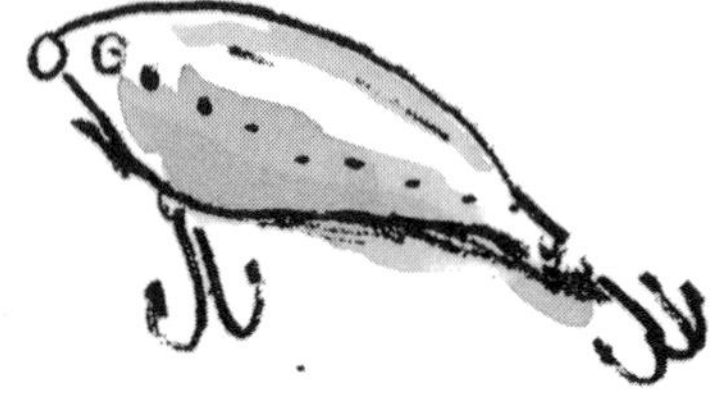

IMAGERY

Imagery helps readers understand what's happening. The imagery in "Crossing the Lake" uses the senses: "Mist sprinkles our arms in dewy drops that glisten in the sun."

INTERJECTION

An interjection is a stand-alone word or phrase that shows how a person feels. In "We Love Fishing," the words "wow!" and "holy cow!" show Dad's excitement. "Gone Fishing" and "Catfish Strong!" also have interjections. If used once in a while, interjections can have a powerful effect in poetry.

METAPHOR

A metaphor is a figure of speech that links two things that are not alike. In "Catfish Sam," the phrase "Torpedo Tough" is a metaphor. Metaphors may not be realistic, and that's how a poet can draw attention to a feeling or thought.

ONOMATOPOEIA

Onomatopoeia is a word that mimics a sound. In "My Big Fish," the word *SNAP!* copies the sound that a person would hear when fishing line breaks. In "Lucy's Quiet Time," *crumples, crunches,* and *slurps* are examples of onomatopoeia.

PERSONIFICATION

Personification is a technique that lets writers pretend that things have human traits. Lucy personifies fish by singing to them in

"Lucy's Song." In "For the Love of Harold, Best of the Worms," Lucy personifies the worm.

REFRAIN

A refrain in poetry is like the chorus in a song. "Winner! Winner!" has the refrain "Winner! Winner! Fish for dinner." A refrain is a phrase that is repeated throughout the poem and can be at the start, in the middle, or at the end of a stanza.

SIMILE

A simile is a figure of speech that compares two different things using the words *like* or *as.* In "Up and at 'Em" Lucy says: "I'll be as quiet as a worm." "A Big Surprise" also has a simile. Similes make a point and, like metaphors, aren't always realistic.

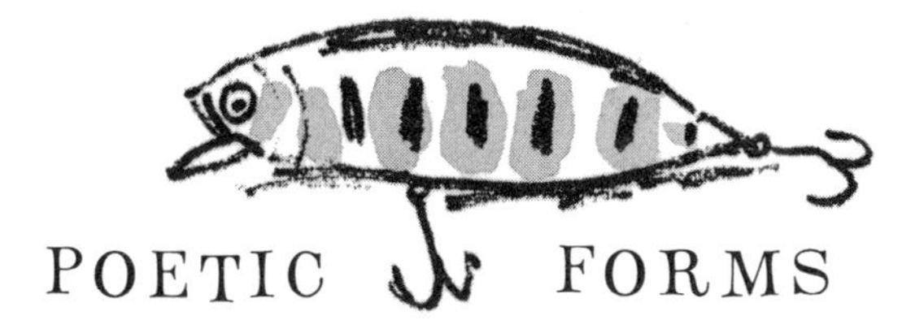

POETIC FORMS

Poetic forms show poets ways to organize and create poems. Some forms rhyme or have a set rhythm pattern. Some forms don't follow a pattern. Instead they will have other guides for writing them, such as ways to describe something or tell a story. There are many poetic forms. This section covers the forms used in *Gone Fishing.*

ACROSTIC POEM

When read down, an acrostic poem such as "Catfish Sam" spells out the poem's subject, usually with the first letter of each line. Acrostic poems grew from a very old poetry form called the abecedarian. In this form, the first letter of the poem's lines or stanzas make up the culture's alphabet from beginning to end. The oldest abecedarian poems are from the Hebrews, who used them when they worshiped. Acrostic poems focus on interesting details.

BALLAD

A ballad tells a short story in verse. "Fishing Flop" follows the spirit of the ballad form. Before there were books, ballads were spoken or sung while listeners danced. The stories were often of bad luck or distress, and sometimes told of gruesome death. Older English ballads were rhyming couplets (stanzas with two lines) that had an iambic heptameter rhythm pattern. *Iambic* means two syllables that have the stress on the second syllable. *Heptameter* means seven sets of syllables. Not all newer ballads follow the traditional form.

BLUES POEM

Blues poems are for one person to sing or speak and often describe a person's sadness or problem. "Can't Go Fishing Yet Blues" is a humorous blues poem written in the style of traditional blues poems. Long ago, African Americans who told stories and sang about their suffering developed blues poems. The poems traditionally have rhyming tercets (stanzas with three lines). Line one is repeated or echoed as line two. Lines one and two rhyme with line three. Blues poems have no set number of stanzas.

CINQUAIN

"Amends" is a twenty-two-syllable cinquain (a stanza of five lines) that doesn't rhyme. It follows a pattern created by Adelaide Crapsey near the turn of the twentieth century. In her pattern, each line has a set number of syllables: two, four, six, eight, and two. The poem is usually a single sentence or thought and, like the haiku, includes an insight. "Next Time" is another type of cinquain stanza.

COMPLAINT POEM

In a complaint poem, the poet criticizes or whines, as Sam does in "Lucy's Quiet Time." Poets may write a complaint poem after a fight with a friend or after having a rotten day. Complaint poems may be long or short, and may or may not have a set rhythm or rhyme.

CONCRETE POEM/SHAPE POEM

The words in a concrete poem are arranged to make a picture of the poem's main subject. "The Night Before Fishing" is a concrete poem. A concrete poem might be long or short depending on the shape the poet is making. This poem doesn't always rhyme or follow a rhythm pattern.

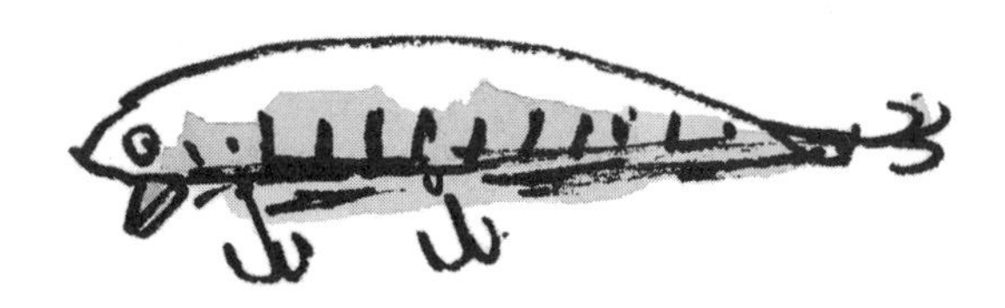

COUNTING POEM

A counting poem such as "Fishing Score" is a traditional poem that does just what it says — it counts. There are many variations of counting poems. The poet can decide how high to count, whether to count up and down or in only one direction, and how to use rhythm and rhyme.

COUPLET

A couplet is a poem, or a stanza within a poem, that has a cluster of two lines. "Gone Fishing" has eight rhyming couplets with short lines. "A Big Surprise" has five rhyming couplets with longer lines. Couplets don't have to rhyme.

CURSE POEM

A curse poem stems from anger or annoyance. As in "A Fishy Spell," this form allows the poet to vent frustration by using lighthearted or goofy exaggerations aimed at someone else. The lines in curse poems should sound like a command and can start with "May," but they don't have to. A curse poem can be short or long and doesn't have to rhyme.

DOUBLE DACTYL

The double dactyl is a short, tricky poem. The first three lines in each stanza have two dactyls (a rhythm pattern with one stressed syllable followed by two unstressed). The last line in each stanza is one dactyl, plus a stressed end syllable that rhymes. Line six or seven is one six-syllable double dactyl word. Anthony Hecht, with help from Paul Pascal and John Hollander, developed this form in the twentieth century. Their form also uses a nonsense word for line one and a person's name for line two, and is one long sentence. "On the Road" follows the spirit of this form.

DRAMATIC POEM

A dramatic poem lets characters speak for themselves and sounds like a conversation when it's performed. Long ago, dramatic poems were written for and performed by a single actor. Today, dramatic poems can be for one character or for several. They can be short or long, and they don't need to rhyme or have a set rhythm. This type of poem is also called performance poetry or poetry for two (or more) voices. "Fishing for Pretend," "Up and at 'Em!," "I See Something," and "We Love Fishing" are dramatic poems.

FORGIVENESS POEM

In a forgiveness poem, a character shows that there are no hard feelings toward another character. It can take any form and may or may not rhyme. "Amends" is a short forgiveness poem.

FREE VERSE POEM

The poet has the freedom to decide the best way to write a free verse poem. It usually doesn't rhyme and it can be short or long. Free verse poems don't have a set rhythm pattern, although poets are careful about how the words sound together when they create these poems. Poets may use a variety of poetry techniques to create free verse poems. "Just Dad and Me," "Crossing the Lake, " "Gulp," and "Just Us Three" are free verse poems.

HAIKU

Haiku is from Japan and has been around for many centuries. It has three lines and often describes something from nature. The whole poem has seventeen syllables, as in "Our Take." The first line usually has five syllables, the second has seven, and the third has five. Poets don't always follow this pattern exactly. To honor the spirit of the haiku, poets use the first two lines to write what they see, and the third line to give an insight about the first two lines. Haiku don't rhyme or have defined rhythmic patterns.

HOW-TO POEM

A how-to poem is a type of list poem that gives creative instructions on how something is done. It may or may not rhyme. "Recipe for Fishing" is a how-to poem written like a recipe.

LIMERICK

The limerick is a short poem that is often funny. As in "Next Time," limericks have anapestic rhythm. That means two unstressed syllables followed by one stressed syllable. Lines one, two, and five rhyme and have three sets of anapests. Lines three and four rhyme and have two sets of anapests. "Once a dad took his daughter and son" is an anapest. Nobody knows for sure how or where the limerick started.

One legend tells how this poem may have been named: Between fights, fifteenth-century Irish soldiers recited poems about their war buddies, then everybody would chime, "When we get back to Limerick town 'twill be a glorious morning."[1]

LIST POEM

A list poems is a descriptive list that defines the poem's subject. Beyond only listing things, though, list poems give specific details about a place, a person, a thing, or an experience so the reader can understand what the poet sees or does. List poems may or may not rhyme. "What to Pack?," "All Aboard!," and "Hooked" are rhyming list poems. "Recipe for Fishing" is an unrhymed list poem formed as a how-to poem.

LYRIC POEM

In a lyric poem a poet expresses thoughts and feelings by writing from a personal point of view. Lyric poems were named after the lyre, a harplike instrument. In ancient times a musician would play a lyre while a poem was sung. The lyric poem may be short or long. It doesn't have to follow a set rhythm or rhyme pattern. "First Catch" and "Fish Tales" are rhyming lyric poems.

MENU POEM

In the menu poem the poet takes a common menu and makes it into a poem. The poet may list the food in an interesting way, or use poetry patterns and comments that wouldn't be on a regular menu. A menu poem may or may not rhyme. "Fish Supper" is an unrhymed menu poem.

NARRATIVE POEM

In a narrative poem the poet tells a story from a third-person point of view, and isn't part of the action. The rhyming poem "Boat Launch" is a variation of a narrative poem that mostly tells how Dad puts

1. Burges Johnson, *New Rhyming Dictionary and Poet's Handbook,* 2nd ed. (New York: Quill/HarperResource, 2001), 37.

the boat in the water. Narrative poems can be about big, important things such as love or war, or something as tiny as a gnat. They can even be nursery rhymes or tall tales, and they may or may not follow a set rhythm or rhyme pattern.

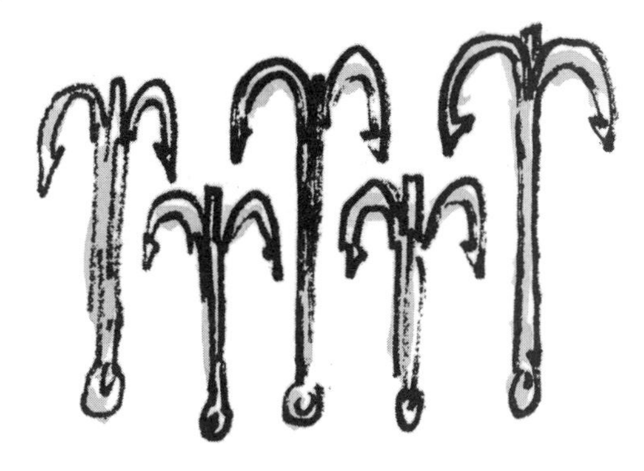

ODE

An ode is a lyric poem that lets the poet express joy about the poem's subject. The first ode is credited to Pindar, a Greek poet who lived more than 2,400 years ago. Pindar wrote victory odes that choirs sang to honor athletes who won in Olympic-type contests. There is no set pattern for newer odes, and they don't have to rhyme. "For the Love of Harold, Best of the Worms" is an ode.

PARODY POEM

A parody poem starts with a well-known poem that someone else wrote. The poet changes most of the words but keeps enough words and patterns so readers can recognize the original poem. "The Night Before Fishing" is a parody poem. It has the same opening and patterns of the familiar story poem "The Night Before Christmas."

POEM OF ADDRESS

In a poem of address the poet "talks" directly to the subject of the poem, although the subject can't usually respond. In "A Fishy Spell" Sam addresses Lucy when she's not there. In "Lucy's Song" Sam explains how Lucy sings to the fish. The whole poem doesn't address the fish, which is why this is a variation of a poem of address. The technique of talking directly to a subject that doesn't respond is apostrophe. Poems of address can be on any subject, and in any form.

PRAYER POEM

In a prayer poem the poet shows support or gives good wishes for something or someone. A prayer poem might be serious or amusing and may or may not rhyme. "Fisherman's Prayer" is a lighthearted prayer poem.

QUATRAIN

A quatrain is a poem or a stanza within a poem that has a cluster of four lines. Quatrains can be written in a variety of rhyme and rhythm patterns, but they don't have to rhyme or have a set rhythm. "When We're Fishing" is a rhyming poem with one quatrain. In each quatrain of "Fishing for Pretend," lines one and three rhyme, and lines two and four rhyme. "My Big Fish" is made of five quatrains in which every other line rhymes. Some lines in this poem have extra breaks that show how Sam battles the fish.

REPRISE POEM

A reprise poem is an echo of an earlier poem. In the reprise poem, some words and patterns can match the earlier poem. The reprise poem isn't an exact copy, though. It needs to reflect how the story has changed. A reprise is different from a parody poem because it echoes a poem that was written by the same poet. "Cleanup" is a reprise that follows the same patterns as "Night Crawlers," but it has different words to show what happened after the fish are caught. "Just Us Three" is a reprise of "Just Dad and Me."

RIDDLE POEM

In a riddle poem the poet gives clues to the poem's subject so the reader can guess the answer. "What Cat Is That?" gives hints about the type of fish Sam catches without giving away the answer.

RONDELET

The rondelet is a short, one-stanza poem with seven lines (a septet). As in "Catfish Strong!," a rondelet has a specific rhyme pattern with only two sets of rhymes. Lines one, three, and seven have four syllables and are a refrain. Line four has eight syllables, and it rhymes with lines one, three, and seven. Lines two, five, and six have eight syllables and rhyme with each other.

SESTET/SEXTET

A sestet is a poem or a stanza within a poem that has a cluster of six lines. It can be made with a combination of couplets, tercets, and/or quatrains. Sestets can be written in a variety of rhyme and rhythm patterns, but they don't have to rhyme or have a set rhythm. "Winner! Winner!" is a rhyming sestet with a refrain.

SWITCHEROO POEM

A switcheroo is a sudden change. A switcheroo poem begins with an interesting topic, then, because of a surprise such as the one in "My Tackle Box," switches to a new topic.

TERCET/TRIPLET

A tercet is a poem or stanza within a poem that has a cluster of three lines. Tercets don't have to rhyme or follow a set rhythm. "Night Crawlers," "Can't Go Fishing Yet Blues," and "Cleanup" are rhyming poems with tercet stanzas. The second stanza in "Catfish Sam" is an unrhymed tercet.

TRIOLET

The triolet is an eight-line poem (an octave stanza) with only two sets of rhymes. Lines one, four, and seven are the exact same line. They rhyme with lines three and five. Lines two and eight are the exact same line, and they rhyme with line six. The thirteenth-century French poet Adeneź-le-Roi wrote the first known triolet. At that time, triolet lines had ten syllables and were on serious topics about heartbreak or loss. Now they are written with six or eight syllable lines and can be funny. "Catching Fish Is Such a Blast!" is a triolet with seven and eight syllable lines.

BIBLIOGRAPHY

Bowkett, Steve. *Countdown to Poetry Writing: Step by Step Approach to Writing Techniques for 7–12 Years*. New York: Routledge, 2009.

Dictionary.com. Dictionary.com, LLC. Accessed May 15, 2011–October 3, 2011. dictionary.reference.com.

Hollander, John. *Rhyme's Reason: A Guide to English Verse*. New Haven: Yale University Press, 1981.

Hughes, Langston. *The Dream Keeper and Other Poems*. New York: Knopf, 1994.

Janeczko, Paul B. *A Kick in the Head: An Everyday Guide to Poetic Forms*. Cambridge: Candlewick Press, 2005.

———. *How to Write Poetry*. New York: Scholastic, 1999.

———. *Poetry from A to Z: A Guide for Young Writers*. New York: Bradbury Press, 1994.

Johnson, Burges. *New Rhyming Dictionary and Poet's Handbook,* 2nd ed. New York: Quill/HarperResource, 2001.

Livingston, Myra Cohn. *Poem-Making: Ways to Begin Writing Poetry*. New York: A Charlotte Zolotow Book–HarperCollins Children's Books, 1991.

Poetryfoundation.org. Poetry Foundation. Accessed August 30, 2011. www.poetryfoundation.org.

Poets.org. Academy of American Poets. Accessed June 15, 2011–September 27, 2011. www.poets.org.

Schultz, Ken. *North American Fishing*. Upper Saddle River: Creative Outdoors, 2007.

Wood, Clement, editor. *The Complete Rhyming Dictionary,* 2nd ed. Revised by Ronald Bogus. New York: Dell Publishing, 1991.